Lunchtime Life Change

Written and Illustrated by
Damon J. Taylor

FOR PARENTS
with Dr. Sock

This story will help children learn that not sharing is wrong, and having Jesus in our lives changes the way we look at life.

Read It Together–

The story of Jesus and Zacchaeus is found in Luke 19:1–10.

Sharing–

Share a time from your childhood that would pertain to this story. Were you ever greedy? Did you have a friend who was greedy?

Discussion Starters–

• Has there been a time when you did or didn't share with a friend?

• Who or what was Zacchaeus' best friend before he met Jesus?

• What does God want us to do with the blessings He gives to us?

• Do you consider Jesus to be one of your friends?

For Fun–

Climb a tree (not too high up) and see how far you can see. While in the tree, retell the story of Zacchaeus and Jesus.

Draw–

Draw with your kids. Have them draw a picture of Zacchaeus in the tree, listening to Jesus.

Prayer Time–

After reading the story, pray with your kids. Thank God for His Son, Jesus. Thank Jesus for being such a kind and loving friend.

COLEMAN HAS FOUND THAT THE LIFE OF A LITTLE BOY

can be tough at times, especially if that boy has a baby sister named Shelby. When Shelby was born, Coleman needed a way to deal with his day-to-day problems. He found his socks. Yes, that's right, his socks.

It may seem weird, but these aren't your regular, everyday tube socks that you find in your dresser. As ordinary as they may appear, these socks really are Coleman's friends, and they help him with his problems. When life gets complicated, Coleman goes to his bedroom and works through his troubles by playing make-believe with his socks and remembering Bible stories he's learned.

So please sit back, take off your shoes and socks if you like, and enjoy Coleman's imaginary world in . . .

Lunchtime Life Change
The Story of Zacchaeus

Coleman's friend Zack was very greedy.

Zack always took the larger piece when Coleman shared his snacks, but Zack never shared his things with Coleman.

Zack climbed up into his treehouse and didn't let Coleman, or any of the other kids in the neighborhood, play with him. Coleman was frustrated with Zack.

"Why doesn't Zack ever share?" wondered Coleman.

Coleman went home to play with his socks.

Out from Coleman's sock drawer popped
Sockariah, one of Coleman's imaginary sock buddies.
"Hey, what's up? You look like something is bugging
you. Why are you so sad?" asked Sockariah.

Coleman told Sockariah about Zack's greediness, and about Coleman's own frustration that Zack never shared anything with anyone.

"Doesn't that remind you of another guy named Zack?" asked Sockariah. "I mean Zacchaeus. The guy in the Bible."

Zacchaeus was a small man. He also had a small heart, and a small group of friends (none, to be exact), but he did have a *large* love for money.

Zacchaeus was a tax collector. He often took more than a fair share of taxes from his neighbors, and kept the extra money for himself. All the people in his town hated him. Even his family had a hard time liking him.

One day at work, Zacchaeus overheard someone talking about a guy named Jesus. They spoke of Jesus' great miracles, His healings, how He loved everyone, and how great a friend He was to everyone.

"I must find out who this Jesus is, and why He is so popular," thought Zacchaeus.
"I wonder if He's paid His taxes yet?"

Zacchaeus wanted to learn more about this Jesus guy. He went to the field outside town, where he had been told Jesus would be.

But he couldn't see anything beyond all of the people who had gathered to hear Jesus speak.

"Why won't these people get out of my way? Don't they know how important it is for me to see Jesus?" Zacchaeus thought.

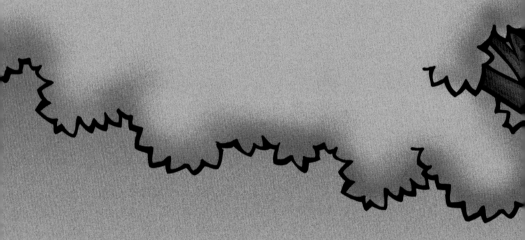

Zacchaeus had a great idea.
"I'm too small to see past all these selfish people, so I will find a way to see over all of them." He climbed up a sycamore tree, and found he could see much better from there.

Once he was settled in the tree, Zacchaeus could see Jesus. He looked just like everyone else, but then again, there was something about Him . . . He seemed happy to see all the people, even the children. He smiled and touched their faces. He spoke of love and kindness. He even talked about being kind to people who didn't deserve it. A few people in the audience turned and looked up at Zacchaeus when Jesus said that.

Jesus' teaching seemed odd to Zacchaeus at first. "Love others like I love myself?" laughed Zacchaeus. "How is that possible?"

Then he understood. Being a loving friend to others, caring for others, and having others care about him—those things were missing in his life.

All his money wasn't making him happy. He was miserable!

Jesus finished His talk, and as He passed underneath the tree Zacchaeus was perched in . . .

IF I CAN'T GET DOWN FROM HERE, I WONDER IF I COULD GET A PIZZA DELIVERED TO THIS TREE.

He said, "Zacchaeus, please come down. Let's have lunch together— at your house!"

The people standing nearby heard this, and they were shocked!

"Jesus just made a lunch date with that horrible Zacchaeus! Doesn't He know how heartless and mean Zacchaeus is?" murmured the townspeople.

"Sure, I'd love to do lunch . . . as soon as I figure out how to get out of this tree," said Zacchaeus.

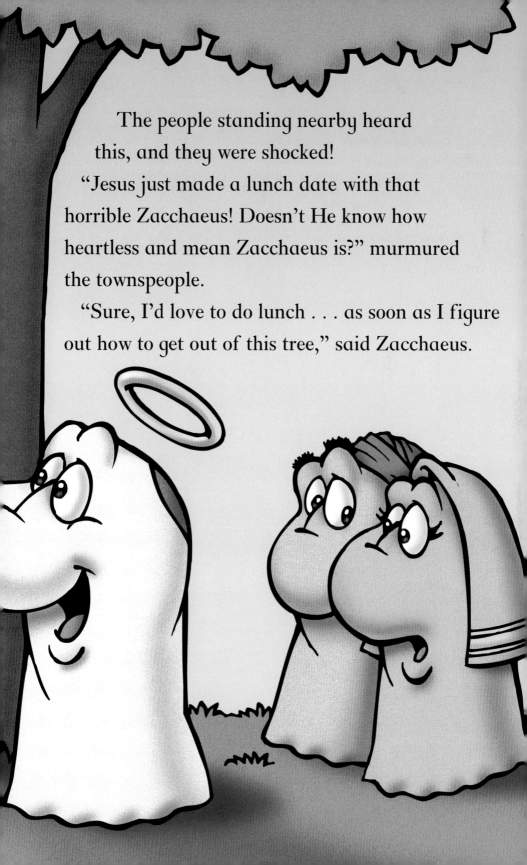

Jesus and Zacchaeus ate lunch together.
This was the first time in a long time
anyone had wanted to eat lunch
with Zacchaeus.

They sat . . . they ate . . . and they talked. That day, Zacchaeus got more than lunch—he received a whole new outlook on life, and he made a new friend.

The next day, Zacchaeus was late for work.
"That's odd," said one of his coworkers.
"Zacchaeus is never late for work. He's here early
every day, inventing new ways to be greedy."

"Come quick! You're never gonna believe this!"
came a voice from down the hallway.

"Zacchaeus is outside giving money back to all the people he stole from, and he's even giving back *more* than he stole!"

Zacchaeus was a new man. Jesus had changed his heart.

"So Coleman, what do you think? Did you learn anything from that story?" asked Sockariah.

"Yep," said Coleman. "If you are gonna climb a tree, you'd better know how to get back down."

"And . . . ?"

"And if I want Zack to be a better friend, I should be an example of what a good friend is, like Jesus was. Jesus wants me to be a caring, sharing, and loving friend to Zack."

"Hey, it's lunchtime. I think I'll ask Zack to come for lunch."

"Good idea, Coleman. Good idea."

The Child Sockology Series